MW00979126

BILLY *the* RESCUE DOG

For Teddy!
♡ Susan
and Billy

WRITTEN BY SUSAN JOYCE ILLUSTRATED BY THEA ERNEST

Maggie's Farm Press | Foster, RI

For all the dogs I've loved; for Cherisse, always;
and for Billy's best friend Gary.
–SJ

In memory of my parents, Nelson and Martha Ernest,
who gave my imagination plenty of room.
–TE

For Akemi, Sophie, Max, Bibi, and Bruno;
for rescuers and rescuees everywhere.
–JC

Published by Maggie's Farm Press, Foster, RI
Printed in Canada by Hemlock Printers
First edition, 2021
For purchase and contact information please visit: billytherescuedog.com

Publisher's Cataloging-in-Publication Data
Names: Joyce, Susan E., author. | Ernest, Thea, illustrator.
Title: Billy the rescue dog / written by Susan E. Joyce; illustrated by Thea Ernest.
Description: Foster, RI: Maggie's Farm Press, 2021. | Summary: A true story of Billy, a Treeing Walker Coonhound,
and his adventures and challenges as he embarks on his new life in his "forever home" on Maggie's Farm in Rhode Island.
Identifiers: LCCN: 2021903871 | ISBN 978-1-7367212-0-9 (hardcover)
Subjects: LCSH Dogs—Juvenile fiction. | Rescue dogs—Juvenile fiction. | Hounds—Juvenile fiction. | Farm life—Juvenile fiction. |
CYAC Dogs—Fiction. | Rescue dogs—Fiction. | Hounds—Fiction. | Farm life—Fiction. | BISAC JUVENILE FICTION / Animals / Dogs |
JUVENILE FICTION / Animals / Pets | JUVENILE FICTION / Lifestyles / Farm & Ranch Life
Classification: LCC PZ7.1 .J69 Bil 2021 | DDC [E]—dc23

Billy is a rescue dog.

Not a dog that rescues
someone lost in the woods...

…or in the snowy mountains.

Maybe it's more accurate to say that Billy is a *rescued* dog.

Billy spent the first year of his life chained to a doghouse.

When some kind people found him, he was sick and very, very thin.

They promised to make him better. And they did.

Once he was healthy, these good people promised to find a family to love him.

And they did.

At first, Billy was overwhelmed.

Everything was new.

He had never met cats.

He had never seen goats...

...or chickens.

Billy had never lived indoors.

He needed time to
get used to everything.

His parents gave him
a bed all his own.

Billy ate breakfast
and dinner, and
lots of treats to
help him get strong.

He took walks with his family.

When the weather grew colder,
Billy wore a new coat to keep warm.

Billy could curl up by the wood stove to nap with the cats,

and lean in for a snuggle,
just to know he was safe.

As Billy settled into his new life, something happened.
He started to find things.

He found a frog.

He found a bunny.

Most exciting of all,
he found a tennis ball.

One day, a fox tried to
grab one of the chickens
for its dinner.

WOOF WOOF
WOOF

The chicken escaped, but Billy's parents couldn't find her.

They searched everywhere.

around the shed
in the woodpile
behind the hen house
up in the apple trees

It was starting to get dark,
and they were getting very worried.

Finally, they turned to Billy and
asked, "Can *you* find the chicken?"

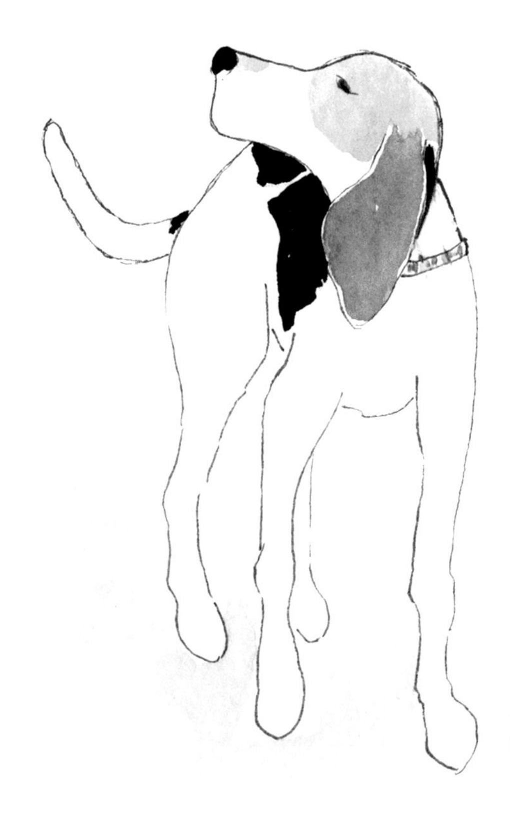

Billy went straight
to a bush and pointed.

And there she was.

The chicken had found
a safe hiding place.

"Billy! You found the chicken!"

It turns out,
Billy *is* a rescue dog.

Billy…

is a Treeing Walker Coonhound. He was rescued from a house where he had been chained outdoors and severely neglected. He was fostered in New England by a kind woman with many dogs until PAWS New England (pawsnewengland.com) found him his "forever home" on Maggie's Farm, in Rhode Island. Billy lives there with his two parents, Susan and Cherisse; a black Lab named Oliver; two cats, Luke and Hazel; three goats, Aria, Gus, and Gwendolyn; and 18 unnamed but well-loved chickens.

Susan Joyce…

writes about life on Maggie's Farm. Billy's story was the first to unfold as a children's book, however there's been some grumbling among the other animals who've lived here longer, so they might have their own books someday.

Thea Ernest…

graduated in metalsmithing from Rhode Island School of Design. She gravitated to painting, and these days you'll find her painting outdoors, all around Rhode Island. She credits her eye for detail to growing up in a family of keen observers. To illustrate Billy's story, Thea studied dogs, cats, goats, chickens, and foxes. She proudly holds the Girl Scout's Dabbler badge.

Jeanette Chow…

is a graphic designer. She's designed pickle jar labels, fair booths, and pages in parenting magazines. Jeanette has been mom to a dog named Barfy and a bunny named Stinky. She currently lives in New York City with lots of adopted plants.

A final note…

Many people made this book possible: Lori and Connie provided expert copyediting and proofreading. Henry, Reilly, Theo, Heidi, Sarah, and Aleta gave invaluable feedback. Manette, Joey, and Katherine shared their expertise. Gosia worked magic on the Kickstarter video; and our supporters touched our hearts. Thank you all.